CHRISTMAS BENEATH THE STARS

A HOLIDAY NOVELLA

❄

MELISSA HILL

CONTENTS

Also by Melissa Hill   vii

Chapter 1	1
Chapter 2	5
Chapter 3	10
Chapter 4	14
Chapter 5	17
Chapter 6	20
Chapter 7	25
Chapter 8	30
Chapter 9	35
Chapter 10	39
Chapter 11	42
Chapter 12	51
Chapter 13	55
Chapter 14	58
Chapter 15	64
Chapter 16	73
Chapter 17	77
Chapter 18	82
Chapter 19	87
Chapter 20	92
Chapter 21	96
Chapter 22	101
Chapter 23	106
Chapter 24	112
Untitled	117

12 DOGS OF CHRISTMAS - EXCERPT

Chapter 1	121
Chapter 2	129
Chapter 3	134
About the Author	141
Also by Melissa Hill	143

Copyright © Little Blue Books, 2020

The right of Melissa Hill to be identified as the Author of the Work has been asserted by her in accordance with the Copyright, Designs and Patents Act 1988.

All rights reserved. No part of this publication may be reproduced, stored in a retrieval system, or transmitted, in any form or by any means without the prior written permission of the author. You must not circulate this book in any format.

All characters in this publication are fictitious and any resemblance to real persons, living or dead is purely coincidental.

ALSO BY MELISSA HILL

Every Little Lie

Not What You Think

Never Say Never

Wishful Thinking

All Because of You

The Last to Know

Before I Forget

Please Forgive Me

The Truth About You

Something From Tiffany's

The Charm Bracelet

The Guest List

A Gift to Remember

The Hotel on Mulberry Bay

A Diamond from Tiffany's

The Gift of A Lifetime

Keep You Safe

The Summer Villa

CHAPTER 1

Hannah Reid loved Christmas.

She loved the cheery feeling in the atmosphere, the twinkling, festive lights and most of all, the sense that at this magical time of the year, anything was possible.

She couldn't add frost or snow to the list though; a born and bred Californian, Hannah wasn't familiar with more traditional wintry Christmas weather.

Yet.

Andy Williams' warm vocals filled the buds in her ears as she reclined in her seat and peered out the window of the aircraft.

Right then, Sacramento lay thousands of miles below in an ocean of darkness and lights. It would be her first holiday season away from home. Her first ever white Christmas.

It was indeed the most wonderful time of the year ...

Hannah hummed the cheery festive tune and glanced down at the cover of the magazine on her lap, a broad smile spreading across her face.

It still felt like a dream.

Discover Wild, one of the biggest wildlife magazines in the country, were sending *her* - Hannah - on assignment.

She ran her hand over the cover shot of a tigress and her cub as they nuzzled together.

It was an amazing photo, one she would have killed to have taken herself.

"Soon," she mused. *Soon it could be my stuff on the cover. All I have to do is get one perfect shot and I'm on my way to a permanent gig with* Discover Wild.

She hugged the magazine to her chest and closed her eyes, relaxing back against the soft leather seat.

IT FELT LIKE JUST A MOMENT, but when Hannah woke it was to the sound of the pilot announcing their descent into Anchorage.

She sat up immediately and looked out the window.

Everything was white!

She'd never seen anything so beautiful. The mountains surrounding the airport were blanketed in thick snow, and a light dusting covered everything else.

She could see the men on the tarmac clearing away the snow, as half a dozen planes in every size - large Boeings to small Cessnas - lay waiting, along with a row of buses to the side.

She wondered which one of those would be taking her to the holiday village she'd chosen as her accommodation while here.

'Nestled deep in the Alaskan wilderness, Christmas World is a true holiday fairytale if ever there was one.

Set amidst lush forest on the South banks of the Yukon River, escape to a magical land where Santa comes to visit every year, and you can find a helpful elf round every corner. Immerse yourself in our idyllic winter paradise and enjoy a Christmas you will never forget ...'

Hannah couldn't wait to experience the true, out and out winter wonderland the online description promised.

Now, the flight was on the ground, but no one

was moving. There was a backup of some sort, and passengers were asked to stay on the plane while it was resolved.

Hannah wasn't too bothered; they'd arrived half an hour early in any case, which meant she still had plenty of time before her transfer.

She preoccupied herself on her phone and more online information and picturesque photographs of Christmas World.

The resort homepage featured a group of happy smiling visitors, with various green-and-red clad elves in their midst.

In the background, picture perfect buildings akin to colorful gingerbread houses dusted with snow, framed a traditional town square. It was exactly the kind of Christmas experience Hannah had always dreamed about as a child.

She couldn't *wait* to be there.

CHAPTER 2

Over an hour later, Hannah was still waiting.

In Anchorage International Airport with forty or so other travellers.

Their Christmas World transfer - the so-called 'Magical Christmas Caravan' was late ... *very* late.

"You can't be serious," a fellow airline passenger commented nearby. "How much longer are we supposed to wait? Are they going to compensate us for this debacle? It is the resort's transport after all," the disgruntled woman asked.

She was surrounded by three miserable-looking children, while her sullen husband stood in a long line of people trying to find out what was going on.

Hannah had noticed the family on the plane earlier, but now she was getting a better look at them. They were exactly the type of people you'd expect to find on such a jaunt; happy family, blonde-haired and blue-eyed, with their cute-as-a-button kids giddy with excitement about a trip of a lifetime to see Santa.

More decidedly *un*happy faces surrounded the resort's airport help desk at the moment, but there were plenty of content ones to be found elsewhere too.

A father with his son excitedly perched on top of his shoulders. A serene mother with her sleeping child, and an elderly couple holding hands while they waited for their connection.

It was everything the holidays should be about, Hannah thought; family and loved ones together at the most magical time of the year.

She had been in plenty of airports, but there was something about this one that appealed to her photographer's eye.

The nearby pillars were like pieces of art, almost abstract; though she didn't really know much about art except what she did or didn't like. These were adorned from top to bottom with garlands and white lights. While elsewhere in the terminal, festive wreaths hung on hooks and there were lots and lots of fresh-smelling pine trees.

And of course, then there was the view....

Hannah had taken countless pictures in her life, some to pay the bills and many more for fun. She'd taken portraits, and even the occasional wedding when things were slow between wildlife jobs, but there was something about the outdoors that she loved most of all.

She'd spent her entire life in it after all, had hiked the Quarry trail in Auburn so many times she felt she knew it by heart. Same for the Recreational River, Blue Heron Trail and the Simpson-Reed Trail, and that was just California.

She'd zigzagged her way across America with her collection of trusty Nikon SLR cameras, but she'd never ventured this far north.

The furthest she'd been was Alberta for a wildlife safari last summer. It was those photos that had opened the door to her current opportunity.

And the reason she was in this snowy picture perfect wonderland right now.

AN HOUR OR SO LATER, and Hannah was peering

out the window of Christmas World's transfer coach as Anchorage melted away in a sea of white.

Fresh snow had begun to fall half an hour before, which almost made up for the exorbitant wait.

But at least they were on their way now, and soon Hannah would have a warm lodge, a toasty fire and the most magical Christmas experience awaiting her.

She wondered if there really would be fresh roasted chestnuts available as advertised, and what kind of activities there would be for guests to enjoy when they arrived.

The website listed things like dog-sledding and carolling, plus places to get hot chocolate, Christmas cookies, and a myriad other festive treats.

All of which sounded amazing, especially since she was tired and in sore need of some holiday cheer after such a long travel day.

She imagined the resort town as something like from the movie, *It's A Wonderful Life,* with that close-knit community feel throughout.

Yes, she was here primarily for a career opportunity, but she'd be lying if she said there wasn't the element of living out a fantasy white Christmas too.

Hannah turned back to the window. The snow was falling harder now, and the smile wouldn't leave her face.

She was about to have the best Christmas ever; she could feel it. And she couldn't wait for it to begin.

It's like Christmas morning. The faster you sleep, the faster it arrives.

Isn't that what Mom and Dad always said?

CHAPTER 3

Two hours later, the coach finally arrived at Christmas World to the applause of all the now-deeply disgruntled and exhausted guests.

It was almost four hours past their scheduled arrival time, and darkness had already fallen hours before; just after two in the afternoon when the sun set.

It was now after seven and Hannah was starving.

It took a while to get off the coach. Everyone wanted to get inside the lodge, but were all too tired to make a mad dash for it, which meant they merely shuffled along as they gathered their belongings.

Though once disembarked, the short walk into the lodge heralded even more long lines.

Hannah's group weren't the only new arrivals this evening, it seemed.

"Oh come on," she groaned.

More lines?

She dropped her camera bag on top of her case as she craned her neck to see as far as the front desk. It was going to be a *long* wait.

"What are they saying up there?" she asked a fellow passenger on the way back from the concierge area.

"They apologized for the delays. Again. It's going to be a couple more hours before our rooms are ready. The hold up with the coaches meant the people checking out were stranded here so things have fallen behind," the older man told her.

"Did they indicate how long of a wait?"

He took a long breath and rolled his eyes. "There's only one person on the desk. By the looks of things, it's going to be a while."

Great.

The man left Hannah to do nothing but wait and take in the madness around her. Everyone looked so exhausted and miserable.

Not exactly a fairytale start.

A porter told everyone to line their bags up along the wall until they were ready to be checked-in.

Hannah left her suitcase, but she wasn't about to leave her camera equipment unattended. She adjusted the strap on her shoulder.

Might be a better idea to just head out and take a look around town instead, maybe take a couple of shots and get a feel for the area?

And perhaps grab a welcome hot chocolate from a cosy cafe...

She gave the long lines one final glance before she stepped out the door and shrugged.

Just because the trip had a poor start didn't mean anything. These things happened in wonderland too.

HANNAH'S BOOT-CLAD feet made barely a track in the snow-covered street, and she felt a childlike thrill as she heard it crunch beneath her steps.

Her footwear matched the tan-colored fur trimmed parka she wore over her light blue jeans, and she pulled a red knit hat from her pocket and put it on, bunching her dark curly hair above her ears.

It was apparently just a couple of minutes walk to the town square from the hotel.

The lodgings at Christmas World seemed to be made up of five buildings, the main hotel and four oversized log cabins that consisted of multiple rooms, each situated amidst spruces on the way in to the centre of town.

Hannah took a few shots of the area as she walked.

The cabins weren't particularly aesthetic or traditional though, and the only lighting along the way came from inside the illuminated buildings.

A cold wind danced across her face. The air was crisp, almost sweet, and she loved it.

The sky was a deep midnight blue and dots of what looked like a million stars filled it. The clarity was remarkable, like nothing she'd ever seen, and certainly nothing at all like the city sky at home.

Hannah raised her camera lens, and the stars immediately rushed into brilliant focus.

Christmas Beneath the Stars... wait 'til Discover Wild *gets a load of this...*

CHAPTER 4

She snapped several shots of the twinkling night sky before going on her way, anticipating more street lighting to appear as she neared the town, but what she saw was not at all what she'd expected.

Harsh fluorescent floodlights illuminated the area around the square. It almost hurt her eyes it was so bright; and just way too much.

Hannah wandered around the square for a while, peering into window after window, her heart plummeting with each consecutive glance.

This place was *nothing* like she imagined. The town square, though pretty, wasn't in the least bit idyllic or magical.

For one thing, it was practically deserted.

The festive lights, smiling visitors, artisan shops and cheerful elves promised in the promo material were all absent.

There was a shabbily dressed (and grumpy-looking) Santa sitting by a cabin and gaudy Christmas tree nearby, taking pictures with unhappy children who weren't at all fooled or indeed impressed by his dingy, fake beard and oversized Santa suit.

Hannah kept walking. Surely there had to be more to Christmas World than *this*?

Eventually, she spied a simple wooden cabin with a red and white sign marked 'Santa's Post Office', which looked interesting.

A bored-looking elf sat just inside it, his head resting on his hand. "Merry Christmas. Leave a letter for Santa. Get one back on Christmas," he recited jadedly.

Her spirits plummeting, Hannah quickly moved on and headed to a nearby 'craft gift' store.

But once again she was disappointed. There were no hand-painted artisan reindeer, woodcraft or any locally-made creations at all.

Instead, she found plastic Santas and inflatable Rudolph toys; the same that could be found at any gift shop in America over the holiday season.

There was *nothing* special about what was on offer there, no souvenirs at all of Christmas World for visitors to take home and treasure.

She frowned. Maybe she was in the wrong area and there was somewhere else - somewhere better?

"Excuse me?" she asked the youthful-looking shopkeeper scrolling through his phone. The kid didn't even look up from the device. "Where are the craft shops? This can't be the only one. Right?"

The kid remained expressionless as he answered. "No."

"No?" she questioned incredulously.

"No." He looked at her as if she belonged in Special Ed class.

She grimaced at a plastic reindeer. "Thanks for nothing," she muttered as she walked away.

She'd had enough for today.

Hopefully her room was ready by now.

CHAPTER 5

Hannah returned to the main lodge to find the reception area now emptying out.

Most of the other guests had been shown to their rooms, and only her belongings remained lined up against the wall.

Thank goodness for that at least. She collected her stuff and headed to check-in.

She'd been assigned an upstairs room, and it was... small.

Hannah expected it to be cosy but not stifling. It reminded her more of a cruise ship cabin than a hotel room.

There was a single bed, a rug and a wooden

chair in one corner of the room alongside a standing lamp.

A bedside table was positioned on the right of the bed with a smaller lamp, alarm clock, and telephone.

There was no TV but she expected that. This kind of destination was all about outdoor activities and fun, not lounging around your room watching cable.

What Hannah didn't expect though was a *picture* of a blazing fire, instead of a fire itself.

But perhaps that was understandable too, what with safety code …?

Still, it was disappointing.

She set her bag on the bed and her stomach growled.

She was still hungry and hadn't actually thought to get anything while she was out.

Nor seen anywhere to tempt her either.

She left her equipment on the bed, grabbed her purse and hurried from the room before it got too late.

Downstairs, she picked up a cold tuna sandwich and a Coke; the best the in-house restaurant could do. Apparently the kitchen closed at eight, and there would be no hot meals until morning.

Hannah couldn't believe it. Still, her rumbling stomach was thankful of *something* at least.

Even so, she decided to head back into town and find a place there. She'd be hungry again in half an hour if she didn't get something else to top-up the sandwich.

She hadn't been away long; half an hour to an hour, maybe a little more, but when she returned to the town square there was … nothing.

The area was now shuttered and in darkness; those awful lights the only thing that remained.

Santa was gone. The post office and souvenir store were closed, along with every other retail unit in the area.

The café? In complete darkness. Even the lights on the Christmas tree at the head of the square were turned off.

So much for winter wonderland. What is this miserable place?

If this was what *real* Christmas was like, Hannah was beginning to suspect she hadn't been missing much.

CHAPTER 6

Her neck and back were aching when she woke the next morning.

Despite an exhausting day's travel, she'd spent most of the night before tossing and turning on the lumpy mattress.

She was also *freezing*.

The radiator in her room was obviously broken, so Hannah spent the night wrapped in a cocoon made out of her bedsheets.

She shuffled to the window. It was still dark out.

"When does the sun come up in this place?" she wondered aloud.

She moved then to the ensuite bathroom, and a few minutes later an ear-piercing scream leaped from her lips as freezing water connected with her skin.

Seemed the water heater wasn't working either!

Hannah checked her camera equipment before she went downstairs for breakfast, lining up all her lenses and hardware and checking everything before she went out.

Once she was dressed, and the camera stuff repacked, she headed to the restaurant for breakfast.

Scrambled eggs, bacon and toast with tea and juice was welcome, but bland and needed a lot of salt and black pepper to make it edible.

She tried to not harp on the growing number of disappointments she was finding at Christmas World, but it was difficult.

There were just so many!

However, she had to remind herself that this trip wasn't just about enjoying the holiday village, ultimately it was about work, and she was determined to get the job done regardless of her dissatisfaction.

Once she got out into the wild, things would surely improve.

. . .

She walked back in to town to find someone who could shed some light on the best vantage points nearby to spot and photograph the Northern Lights.

It was pretty apparent last night that the artificial street lighting here gave off way too much light pollution for anyone to spot the phenomenon from the town.

Hannah zipped up her jacket and headed back out with two bags of equipment; her usual camera bag and another containing additional lenses.

She saw a line of people forming just up ahead as she passed a sign that read SLED & SLEIGH RIDES.

Hmm... The idea of an actual sleigh ride through the snow, pulled by genuine reindeer was so tempting. She'd always wanted to experience that.

"Wanna take a ride?" a nearby attendant asked her. She was pleasant, but Hannah got the feeling that the woman wasn't very enthusiastic about being there.

She was dressed as an elf but she had to be at least sixty years old. She actually reminded Hannah of her grandmother.

"Are those ... real reindeer?" she asked in an almost childlike tone, her anticipation building.

The woman chuckled. "Yes, they are. Would you like to take a ride? It's only fifty dollars. It takes you into the forest around town and a little further north too."

"North?" Hannah questioned. "Could you see the aurora borealis from up there?"

"Maybe," the woman shrugged. "The lights can be a bit unpredictable. They happen when they want to. So what about that ride?"

Hannah contemplated the prospect for a moment. "Sure. I'll take it. I just need to check something first," she added.

There was an information desk close by too.

If anyone would know where best to find the Northern Lights someone there surely would. That way, if the sleigh ride took her close enough, she could get her shots and enjoy some fun at the same time.

She approached the kiosk.

"Hi there," Hannah greeted with a smile as she walked up to the tourist information window.

"Hi. You, uh ...want to write a letter to Santa?" a young man questioned with a raised brow. It was the same bored kid Hannah had seen the evening before. He caught himself a second after saying it. "Sorry. I mean, Christmas World Information - how can I help?"

She chuckled lightly. The man in red she saw the night before was no Santa, and even if he was, she wouldn't write to him. "I need a local guide. I want to go see the aurora borealis." She smiled.

The elf looked at her, confused. "Aurora borealis?"

"Yes," Hannah replied. "You know...the Northern Lights?"

"I know what you mean," he replied. "I just don't know anyone who can help you. The lights happen when they want to. No one can be sure when. You might see them a bit further north maybe, but where exactly, I dunno. I've never actually seen them myself."

She blinked in surprise. "But you live around here, don't you? How can you not know where to find them?"

He shrugged. "I don't really have any reason to leave town. Everything is here."

Hannah sighed. This truly was just getting better and better...

CHAPTER 7

"OK thanks anyway," she muttered.
"Have a nice day."

She wandered back to the sleigh ride area only to be met by a very long line of waiting people.

Nearby, a group of husky dogs skidded away, with a group sitting happily in the sled behind them.

But there were so many people ahead of her for the reindeer ride, and with the length of time it took for one group to go around and come back, Hannah figured it could well be *hours* before she got her turn.

She stood in the line for a few more minutes before she got tired of it.

"This is ridiculous," she muttered. The man in front of her turned back in jaded agreement.

There was no point in just standing around for ages, wasting her day. There *had* to be a better way to get out into the forest to find the phenomenon, and if it meant finding it on her own, then so be it.

Hannah marched back to the information desk. "Where can I rent a snowmobile?" she demanded.

The attendant looked at her as if she were annoying him and Hannah resisted the urge to give him some Californian sass.

She didn't know why she was surprised though. What was poor customer service when it came to this place? Everything about it was lacklustre and disappointing.

"There's a place over on the other side of town," he droned.

"How much?"

"Twenty bucks an hour, I think."

"Thank you" Hannah replied imperiously, before hurrying away in the direction he pointed.

She had a snowmobile to catch.

FIFTEEN MINUTES LATER, she was packing her

equipment onto the back of a fluorescent green Polaris.

The attendant gave her a matching helmet for safety.

"Are you sure you can handle that thing?" the young guy asked.

"Yeah, I'm sure," she scoffed, as she put the helmet on and started it up.

She turned the heavy machine around and headed north, thankful to be leaving the dreary town and letting those garish spotlights fade into the background.

They spoiled everything. The few shots she'd taken the night before were horrible. Overexposed and distorted.

The engine revved in Hannah's ears as she raced across the sea of white. There were several trees on the path but they were so well-dispersed it made navigation easy.

The light was beginning to come up and she was sure that if she traveled far enough she'd find the lights on her own once darkness hit again later. She just wasn't sure how far, but knew to keep careful track of where she was going just in case.

She'd hiked enough and lost her way enough back home to know what to do.

Though Alaska was different. It was dark twenty hours of the day, and of course mostly white on the ground, which meant keeping track was a little more difficult, but not impossible.

Thanks to the stars.

Her late father had taught Hannah from an early age how to find her way by the stars.

All she had to do was find the North Star. It was at the tip of the Little Dipper's handle, the first constellation her dad had ever shown her.

She felt a pang, missing him afresh.

He would love it here out in the forest. This is just his kind of thing.

She smiled to herself. Her father had been an adventurer. He'd sparked it inside of her and it was a flame that had never been extinguished.

She'd taken him on many of her wildlife shoots in return. It was only later in life that he'd stopped going. When rheumatoid arthritis started it was difficult for him to accept that he could no longer do the things he used to.

And while he was now longer around to do the things they loved, Hannah still could, and she would.

It was her dream for so long. She wasn't going to let anyone or anything stop her.

She was going to find one of the world's most amazing natural phenomena.

Hanah would stay out here in the snow, beneath the sky for as long as needed, until she could capture the aurora borealis in a way that would immortalize it forever.

No matter what.

CHAPTER 8

Alaska cold was like none other Hannah had ever experienced, however.

Her breath didn't come out as mist, but as an actual cloud before her eyes.

Thankfully she had goggles to protect them from the blinding glare of the sun bouncing off the blanket of white.

The tundra was spectacular though; the snow drifts all-encompassing. There didn't seem to be a single spot uncovered out there.

The shifting winds drew patterns in the snow like a finger. It all looked like a patchwork quilt from the distance, and Hannah kept stopping the snowmobile to photograph the almost surreal landscape.

The sun appeared just after eleven am, but by three-thirty it was setting again.

Hannah took as many photos as she could during daylight hours, but of course it was in darkness that she'd have the best hope of tracking down the auroras.

Now the sky was truly dazzling, studded with stars that looked like diamonds overhead.

She got off the snowmobile and set her goggles and helmet aside to just look up and stare at it.

She wandered slightly, allowing her feet to carry her as her eyes remained focused above her.

Just incredible ...

She stayed there immobile, completely oblivious to what may lurk in the trees or in which direction she was walking. She just kept following the patterns in the stars, letting them be her guide.

I should have come here long ago. It's like an untouched land ... as if nothing has changed here since the world began.

Eventually Hannah returned to the snowmobile and placed her goggles and helmet back on before heading north.

The attendant said that was the way to go, so that was where she was going.

. . .

An hour later she was further north, but still no closer to spying the aurora borealis.

She'd searched in every direction she could think of and still there was nothing.

Could a phenomenon hide? Wasn't it supposed to be right there, for all to see?

Hannah flipped her goggles up over her helmet and looked around her. Where else could she look?

This was her future, the biggest opportunity of her professional life; she needed to find the Northern Lights soon.

She *had* to.

She took a few more shots of the twinkling night sky, but another hour or so later there was still no sign of what she'd come to see.

She sighed and leaned on the handles of the snowmobile. What was she going to do? Clearly she was in the wrong place, or the conditions weren't right, or *something*.

The problem was she needed to figure this out. She wasn't going to get another opportunity like this. It could make or break her career.

She decided to give herself one more hour before giving up.

But still, there was still nothing.

Hannah set her helmet on the handle of the snowmobile and took a long, deep breath.

She felt tears of frustration sting her eyes, but quickly pushed them back.

"You are not gonna panic," she told herself. "There's always tomorrow. You'll be able to find *someone* in town who knows about the auroras, and they can point you in the right direction. You are not a quitter. You never have been. Just get back to town and start afresh tomorrow."

She gave the sky one last glance before she put the helmet back on and restarted the snowmobile.

The engine had just stirred to life when tiny flecks of snow began to fall, immediately lightening Hannah's mood.

I really could just stay in this picture postcard forever...

She took a few artistic shots of snowflakes against the sky with the moon and stars in the background, before she reluctantly put the camera away, and manoeuvred the snowmobile round to head back.

The weather began to come down even harder and a few minutes later, her vision was almost completely obscured.

In the blizzard, Hannah truly couldn't tell where she was going and had nothing to guide her.

Snow clouds hid her trusty stars, and every tree she passed seemed just like the other.

She stopped the vehicle to help gather her bearings, trying not to panic. The snow was coming down way too hard. It was a risk to keep going so better to just wait a little until it eased off.

Hannah sat impatiently on her snowmobile for a half hour or so until the heavier snowfall eventually lightened.

When all was clearer she once again tried to find her way back to the resort village.

But her earlier tracks were completely gone by now, the fresh snowfall obscuring her only means of finding her way back.

Things truly were just going from bad to worse ...

CHAPTER 9

Hannah's gaze searched frantically around. Which way?

She bit the inside of her cheek as she contemplated one direction over another.

She drove slowly and with trepidation, hoping for some confirmation that she was going the right way, until finally passing a clump of trees that looked familiar.

Relieved she was on the right track, she turned up the throttle, eager to get back now.

She was getting hungry, not to mentioned wet, tired and *cold*.

In her haste, she steered the vehicle round a cluster of trees, going far too fast.

Hannah felt the big machine begin to slide, right in the direction of a large snow-covered mound of ... something.

Her eyes grew large as she realized she was going to hit it. Swerving in panic, she felt the snowmobile begin to give way and topple over, and like a mother protecting her children, she reached for her camera bag to save it.

She squeezed her eyes shut as she tumbled free of the snowmobile and landed awkwardly in the snow.

Feeling a sharp pain in her wrist, Hanna cried out, her hand clasped around it. She hissed, the pain of it throbbing through her as she rocked back-and-forth.

It took several minutes before the pain eased enough for her to release her hold.

With the other hand, Hannah unbuckled her helmet and removed it so to assess the damage to herself, the snowmobile, but most importantly, her camera equipment.

She felt no pain anywhere else except for her wrist, and for that much she was thankful.

Her cameras seemed to be all in good order too; however, the snowmobile on its side half-buried beneath a snow mound was not so lucky.

The problem was, with her injured wrist, there was no way she was going to be able to dig it out on her own to get back.

Which meant she was stranded. Deep in the forest in the darkness amid falling snow - all on her own.

Hannah looked around again as panic began to creep into her heart. She grabbed her phone from her bag and began to dial the number for the Christmas World lodge.

No service.

She tried again, but the call still refused to go through. Her fears began to grow the longer the line refused to connect.

She was stranded in the dark, in the middle of nowhere without a single way of communicating her situation to anyone.

What was she going to do? She had enough snacks and water to last a couple of hours at least, and her clothes were thick enough to keep her warm enough for a while ... but she had nowhere to shelter if the snow started falling again, nor knew anywhere nearby to take refuge.

Hannah got to her feet, her hand cradling her aching wrist. She turned around, searching for some kind of magic answer to her problem, but there was nothing.

No sign of anything. No smoke rising into the air, no sound except a light wind in the trees.

CHAPTER 10

"Hello?" she called out impulsively. "Anyone there?"

Silence.

Her heart began to stampede.

Be calm, Hannah. Be calm.

She wandered clear of the tree line.

Maybe if she got into a clearing she might be able to see better? Perhaps there was something on the way that she'd missed...

Her feet sunk into the snow up as far as her calves. She shivered, more out of fear now than cold.

Then she thought she heard something in the distance. Something faint, and her hearted quickened even more.

"Hello!" she called out again, this time much louder. "Anyone?"

Her eyes searched the tundra for some sign of which direction the noise was coming from.

Then she heard it again, a little louder this time. Then again, and this time she could make out what it was.

Dogs barking.

Her heart began to fill with hope. If there were dogs out here, then there must be somewhere close by for her to find safety.

Hannah cupped her good hand against her mouth and yelled as loudly as she could. "Hello!"

She spotted it then, a sled led by six husky dogs and a single driver.

She moved towards it, waving her good hand frantically as she continued to call out.

It took a minute before she was noticed, but mercifully the sled eventually started in her direction.

Her heart almost leaped out of her chest with relief.

She was safe.

Hannah walked toward the stranger, who would surely help get her back to civilization.

"Hey there, can you help me? I had an accident," she said, approaching the stranger, just before another thought stuck her.

Please, please don't be a serial killer...

CHAPTER 11

Hannah's heart was still beating hard in her chest, as the sled driver approached.

She dismissed the fear as she glanced at the adorable huskies leading it. There were six altogether, and she stepped closer as the dogs came to a stop.

Her eyes drifted from the animals to their master. A guy was standing on the back of the sled, an earflap hat on his head and large goggles covering his eyes.

Breath billowed from his lips as he looked at her. Then he stepped off the sled and raised the goggles from his face.

Hannah's heart fluttered.

This guy was made to be photographed. The camera would devour him (along with likely every woman who got an opportunity).

His face was tanned with an angular jaw, full lips, light green eyes, and she could see golden-blonde hair peeking out from beneath his hat.

He was tall too, at least a foot taller than she was, and dressed in a dark parka and thick ski pants.

If she had to guess, he wasn't from around these parts, not with that tanned complexion, but he'd definitely dressed for the weather.

"What happened here?" he asked as he approached. He removed his gloves and stuffed them into his pocket. "Anyone else out here with you?"

His question did cause Hannah a little apprehension. Was she alone?

Stop ... overactive imagination.

"No, it's just me. I was trying to get back to town and I took a turn too quickly and my snowmobile turned over in a snowbank," she explained. "It's back there in the trees."

"It happens. I'm Bruno. Bruno Locke," he introduced himself.

"Hannah Reid," she replied. Forgetting herself,

she instinctively flexed her wrist to take his hand, but the moment she did, a shot of pain ran up her arm.

She grabbed at her wrist again to soothe it.

Please, don't be broken. Don't be broken.

"You OK?" Bruno questioned.

She grimaced. "I hurt my arm when I fell off the snowmobile. It's nothing."

He stepped closer and took her hand. She could see the slight shadow of a mustache over his lip and she averted her eyes, and instead tried to focus on what he was doing with her arm.

He moved her wrist around, first to the left and then the right, and finally up and down. She hissed her displeasure as fresh pain coursed through her.

He cocked an eyebrow. "Sounds like more than 'nothing' to me," he commented, then glanced at the snowmobile, emblazoned with the Christmas World logo. "You staying at the resort?"

Hannah nodded.

"It's late. Better get you back soon." He released her hand and started walking to where she'd fallen. "What were you doing all the way out so far this late?"

Hannah grimaced. "I was actually trying to see the aurora borealis, but I couldn't find it."

His brow wrinkled slightly. "The auroras? You won't see anything out this way. Didn't anyone tell you?"

"No," she said through gritted teeth. "I tried to find someone to show me but the people in that ... town didn't seem to have a clue. They told me to head further north, so here I am."

"Folks who live up here with the auroras don't find them as impressive as those who come from far away." Bruno looked her over. "And by the looks of you, I'd say you come from very far away."

"California," she informed him. "I'm out here on a work assignment."

He walked ahead of her, his long strides allowed him to move a lot faster than Hannah. He looked over his shoulder. "What do you do?"

"Photographer," she replied.

He reached the snowmobile and Hannah occupied herself with collecting her scattered belongings, while he worked on getting her transportation free.

She stood watching as he began to dig the snowmobile out. It didn't take him long with two perfectly working hands, though it did take a little more effort to get it upright again.

"Do you need help?"

"I think my hands are better than yours at this point," he replied. "I just need to get a little leverage."

Bruno lowered himself and used his body weight to push the snowmobile over. It took him a couple of tries, but eventually he got it done.

"Thanks." Hannah stepped closer and inspected the snowmobile with him. It seemed OK on the surface, the body undamaged at least.

Bruno got into the seat and tried to start it.

The engine made a strange sound but didn't turn over. He tried again. Same thing.

"Sounds like your engine's flooded," he commented. "There's no way you're getting back to town on this thing."

"So what do I do? I can't just stay out here…"

He smiled, a wide grin that displayed perfectly even, polished white teeth, and dimples to boot.

"Well, you definitely need to get someone to look at that wrist soon. I can give you a ride back." Bruno got off the snowmobile, took the keys out of the ignition and handed them to her. "You staying at one of the lodges?"

"Yes, the main lodge at Christmas World. The most *un*-Christmassy place you can possibly imagine," she muttered, rolling her eyes. "Honestly, it's more like somewhere you want to *avoid* if you want to retain your Christmas spirit. But unfortunately, I'm stuck there until I get this job done."

Bruno nodded silently. "Most un-Christmassy place huh?"

"Yes. You've heard of Christmas World I take it?"

"Yeah, I've heard of it. It was quite a place years ago but now it's something else."

"Ha! *That's* an understatement," Hannah scoffed as she did her best to get her haversack and camera bag over her shoulder. "I came here expecting this amazing once in a lifetime festive experience," she admitted. "I thought it was going to be the Christmas I never had. And I was right - but in *all* the *wrong* ways."

Her heart sank as the words left her lips. She didn't truly admit to herself how disappointed she was by Christmas World until she'd uttered the words out loud.

She looked at her feet as they sank into the snow. "I thought I was going to have my first perfect white Christmas, while also getting to experience one of the world's most amazing natural phenomena. Instead, I was met with the polar opposite. Plus I can't seem to even find the Northern Lights."

"Let me," Bruno offered. He slid both bags from her shoulders and started walking toward the sled. "I'm so sorry you were disappointed."

She shrugged. "It doesn't matter I guess. I'll make the most of it. If I get the shots I came for, then it'll be worth it."

"What if you don't? That wrist doesn't look so good."

"Then I'm looking forward to the *worst* Christmas imaginable, cooped up in Scroogeville while I wait for this to heal." She waved her injured hand slightly. "This is nothing. Just a little bump. I'm sure it'll be fine in a day or two." She looked back at the snowmobile. "Though I can't just leave that there, can I? The rental place is gonna want it back."

"I've saved the location on GPS. They'll be able to send someone to retrieve it. Now, take a seat," Bruno declared. He'd cleared a place in front of him on the sled for her to sit.

Hannah patted the dogs and they licked her hand. Two of them were black and white, another two were copper-red and white and the last two were paler versions of the ones before. They were all so adorable with their pale eyes. One had heterochromia: one eye pale blue and the other ochre.

"These guys are so sweet," she stated as she knelt beside the dogs and gave them an additional pat on the head each. They jumped up playfully. "I always wanted dogs like these," she added.

"I always wanted them too," Bruno agreed. He smiled. "That's why I got them."

Hannah got up and walked to the sled, lowering herself onto it.

"Pull the blanket over your legs. It'll get pretty cold being closer to the snow."

She did as Bruno suggested. "What're their names?"

"The three on the left are Bonbon, Snicker and Tootsie. The other three are Caramel, Chocolate and Vanilla," he told her, as he gave the command and the dogs started off running.

Hannah chuckled. "You have a sweet tooth?"

"Just a little. How could you tell?"

She took the liberty of peeking over her shoulder at him. The goggles were back in place but it did nothing to detract from the fact that he was a seriously good-looking guy. She wondered how he'd ended up all the way out there in the wild.

"Let's get you home."

"Whoopee," Hannah said lackluster. "Christmas World here we come."

She wrapped her arms around her knees deep in thought, as the tundra began to fly by.

She had no idea how she was going to explain the accident to the attendants at the rental place, or the additional eighty bucks she owed them for staying out far longer than she'd promised.

No Northern Lights. No pictures. Busted snowmobile. Busted wrist.

Could this trip truly get any worse?

CHAPTER 12

❄

The town was unsurprisingly, once again in darkness when they approached.

A deep sigh left Hannah's lips at the sight of it. Didn't anyone ever tell whoever ran Christmas World that activities and lights - *especially* during the holidays - might be good for business?

What was it with these people?

"See what I mean?" she commented to Bruno archly. "This is supposed to be a magical, festive destination, yet the place is in complete darkness before anyone even has a chance to get out and enjoy it. It's just so ... *depressing*! Especially when it's dark up here so many hours already, and when you look out your window there's only more darkness. To say nothing of those tacky fluorescents in the square …"

Bruno murmured agreement as he steered the dog sled up to a darkened building.

"Wait here," he instructed. "I'll go get a doctor."

Hannah looked at him surprised. "Where will we find a doctor now? Everywhere's closed."

He removed his hat and goggles, and she realized that she was right about his model good looks. His tousled golden-blonde hair fell just above his ears. He looked like a Norse god.

She swallowed hard.

"I know a guy, Dr. Morgan who lives out this way. I'll go get him and bring him back." He switched on a lamp strapped to the back of the sled. "So you won't be alone in the dark," he added as he flashed a smile. "And the dogs will be here to keep you safe. You don't have to worry though, we don't really have any crime up here. Everyone knows everyone else so it doesn't leave much room for mischief."

With that, he strode off into the darkness and Hannah remained with the dogs.

The pups began playing the moment they were left on their own. They tumbled over each other and wrestled like children. She smiled. So far, they (and Bruno) were the best thing about this place.

She got to her feet with some pain and effort; her wrist was throbbing terribly as she moved, and she aggravated it even more when she tried to get up from her low seating.

Hannah held it to her chest as she looked again around the deserted town. Why did they even *bother* to promote this place as a vacation destination?

Like Jurassic Park at Christmas, she grumbled. Minus the dinos.

Nearby the reindeer were milling around in their pen. The wind was blowing gently through the trees and the smell of spruce filled the air.

Though if they *did* do something with the place it could be amazing….

Hannah turned back to focus her attention on the dogs. They were a friendly little bunch and didn't seem alarmed or wary of her at all, not even with Bruno gone. They seemed to like her as much as she liked them.

Minutes more passed and soon their owner was returning, with another man beside him. "Doc, this is Hannah, the guest I told you about."

The hefty man smiled at her. "The little snow-racer," he mused. He stepped toward her and looked at how she was cradling her arm. "Let's get you inside so I can get a better look at what we're dealing with."

CHAPTER 13

In truth, Hannah was a bit shocked by what she found inside the town Medical Centre.

Christmas World in general might have been a dud, but their healthcare facilities were obviously top notch.

Unfortunately for Hannah, that didn't necessarily mean anything good for her.

"It's a sprain, and a bad one. Grade Two. This means that some of the palmar ligaments have partially been torn," Dr. Morgan explained. "You're going to have some loss of function, and you're going to need to have your hand immobilized in a splint for at least a week." He went over to a supplies cabinet and began to unpack items from it. "I'll give you some stretching exercises to help regain your mobility."

Hannah's heart fell through the floor. "Doctor … are you telling me I won't be able to use my hand at all?"

This couldn't be happening. If she couldn't use her shooting arm then there was no way she was going to complete her photography assignment.

"Isn't there any way to speed up this process? I mean, a painkiller or something? I really need to use my arm. It's work."

"I'm sorry. There's truly no way to rush these things. It takes as long as it takes."

Hannah was silent as Dr. Morgan wrapped her arm.

None of it seemed real. She couldn't locate the auroras, she had a sprained wrist, and was marooned in the worst 'holiday destination' imaginable.

This has to be some kind of joke. Or definitely a bad dream.

When the doctor was finished, she returned to the reception area where Bruno was still waiting.

"So what's the verdict?"

"A bad sprain," Dr. Morgan answered.

"At least it's not broken."

"No, just injured enough to ruin everything I came here for," Hannah grumbled. "I better get back to the lodge and get a message to the magazine, let them know what happened and that I can't complete the assignment."

She strode toward the door, determined to walk off her disappointment and frustration.

Though Bruno stepped in front of her, and touched her arm gently.

"Hannah, I don't think you should go back to the lodge yet," he stated. "The magazine can wait until tomorrow when you've had time to process what's happened. You're upset right now; not the best state of mind to figure out what you need to."

"I'll be fine," she protested.

"Look, I know a place. Let me take you for some hot chocolate to cheer you up? You've had a lousy day."

"Bruno…"

"I won't take no for an answer," he insisted.

He flashed a grin in her direction, and Hannah knew it would be rude to refuse, especially when he'd been so kind already.

Not to mention she couldn't resist a smile like that even if she tried.

CHAPTER 14

Bruno led her outside, and back to the sled.

He drove it a little way across the town square to one of the few places with lights on; a tiny café with no more than six tables inside.

It had large picture windows lined halfway with a short white curtain. Ornate electric starlights hung at the top, casting pretty light patterns on the walls.

They left the dogs outside, and upon entering, Hannah was surprised to find that a proper working fireplace was providing most of the heat. Two large, plush chairs sat on a cosy rug by the hearth.

A woman stepped out from behind a counter

the moment they entered. She had pepper and salt hair that hung in a thick braid over her shoulder. Her skin was olive, and there was such youthful vigor in her movements that it made Hannah smile.

"Hey, Bruno. I haven't seen you here in a while. How's your dad?" she asked, as he attempted to help Hannah out of her coat. "What happened here?" she added, indicating her sling.

"Thanks Gretta. Dad's good. I know it's late, but my friend here needs some of your famous hot chocolate." He flashed that grin again, one that would melt any woman's heart.

"Famous, huh?" she replied, an amused twinkle in her eye. "You can take that table over by the window." She looked at Hannah. "You hungry sweetheart?"

"Starved."

"Then I'll bring you guys a menu too. Get yourselves comfortable; I'll be right back."

They sat at the table and Hannah stared down at her wrist. She was so disappointed, but for Bruno's sake tried to distract herself. "She seems lovely."

"Yep. Gretta owns this place and she is. Her family has been in this area for two hundred years.

They were some of the original tribes in the area before it became settled."

"That's amazing."

"The cafe is here since before I was born," he continued. "The family have been taking care of the people round here ever since, and the café was just Gretta's addition to that legacy. Plus, she makes the best food between here and Anchorage." Then his expression fell. "Hannah, I'm afraid I owe you an apology."

She frowned. "What? You don't need to apologize for anything. None of this is your fault."

"Actually it is," he replied.

She stared at him, confused. "What are you talking about?"

"There's something I should tell you. When you asked if I'd heard of Christmas World, and I said I did. Well ... it's a little bit more than that. I own it."

Her eyes widened, stunned. "You ... own it?"

"Pretty much. I'm the CEO. I took over running the company last year when I came back from the military. My father was sick and he passed on the management to a third party while I was away, but when he got worse I took early leave to come home."

Her jaw dropped as she listened. Then she

snapped it closed and played off the action with a lick of her lips.

"I...I don't know what to say. I'm kind of embarrassed obviously. I would never have said what I did if I..."

"Knew?" Bruno finished. He smiled. "It's alright. You were just being honest. Besides, I needed to hear it. I can't pretend this place is anything like it used to be."

Hannah leaned closer. "What happened? Forgive me for being nosy, but this isn't at all what I imagined and definitely isn't what's advertised. I don't want to believe you'd trick people into coming here, so something must have happened to turn the place into...well into this."

"Here you go," Gretta interrupted politely. She set two large mugs in front of them, filled with rich chocolate, whipped cream and marshmallows on top. It smelled divine.

"Thanks, Gretta. This looks great," Bruno smiled. "It's always great here," he said to Hannah.

"I wish there were more people who thought so," the woman replied glumly. "Things have been so slow this year."

"I know."

Hannah could see the disappointment in Bruno's expression.

"Things will probably pick up closer to Christmas though," Gretta assured him quickly. "Every town has its ups and downs. We've made it through worse and we will make it through this one." She patted his shoulder comfortingly. "I'll let you both decide on what you want to eat."

Gretta left them and Bruno turned back to Hannah.

"See, it isn't just you who thinks this place isn't what it used to be. Everyone does. The company my dad had taking care of things made some big mistakes. Letting staff go to reduce costs, closing early to reduce expenses, and raising prices on retail space to increase profit. What it did was force all of the artisans out, left local people without work, and turned Christmas World into … a crackerjack house." He sipped his chocolate and set it aside. "They thought that 'recreating daylight' with those floodlights you hate was more cost-effective than the lighting system already in place."

"They sure got that wrong."

"Yes, they did. So I do feel personally responsible for the awful time you're having here. And the guys who rented the snowmobile really should've given you a map too, but they sent you off unprepared. You came here for a dream Christmas but got a nightmare instead."

Hannah's gaze fell to the table. She felt so bad for him and doubly terrible for complaining so vociferously earlier. He'd already done so much to help her today, and he didn't even know her

"Truly it's not your fault." She placed her good hand on his to get his attention. "Maybe my expectations were just too high. Yes, things might have gotten off to a bad start around here. But I have a feeling they'll get better."

He met her gaze then and something ... Hannah couldn't be sure what, passed between them.

She felt her cheeks grow warm, worried that she'd overstepped, then pulled her hand away and picked up her oversized mug with her good arm.

She raised a toast. "Here's to starting over."

Bruno smiled and raised his in return.

CHAPTER 15

Hannah regarded Bruno over the brim of her oversized cup, still feeling like such a heel for what she'd said, and the obvious discomfort it had brought him.

"Hey," she said softly then. "I know you said I don't have to, but I really do want to apologise too. I'm very sorry for what I said about this place. I had no right to go off on you like that before. I should've just kept my big mouth shut. I feel like I insulted you and your family business and that was not my intent. It really wasn't."

He smiled at her. "You told the truth. As I said, I appreciate honesty and I share your views. This isn't the type of place people would want to come back to, which is probably why they haven't."

"I heard what Gretta said. Christmas World is in trouble?"

Bruno nodded. "Since my father retired, visitor numbers and satisfaction have been plummeting a little more each year. Eventually, I don't think they'll be anything left of it," he admitted glumly.

She looked to where Gretta had disappeared to. The woman was still behind closed doors in the back.

It made Hannah feel she could ask her next question without reserve. "Do you mean the resort is in danger of closing?"

He sighed heavily. "It was a mistake allowing anyone but my family to take care of this place. My great-grandfather founded Christmas World you know. He wanted a place where it could be Christmas every day."

A soft chuckle left his lips, and Hannah found herself smiling as she listened to him.

"You ever realize how everything seems brighter and better at Christmas?" His light green eyes lit up as he spoke. "It's as if nothing bad could happen. My great-grandfather wanted to try and keep that feeling all year round. What better way than to create a place where it really could be Christmas every day?"

"This place is like this all the time?" Hannah was incredulous. She thought the resort was just for the holiday season.

"Not any more, but it used to be," Bruno replied, his eyes shifting away from her.

She truly didn't know what to say. Yes, initially she felt as if she'd been almost tricked into coming to Christmas World, and that the place closing was surely better than letting it keep going the way it was.

But that was before she'd met Bruno. He wasn't some manipulative, money-hungry capitalist exploiting people's hard-earned money and expectations.

He was a former soldier - a man who'd fought for their country - who'd taken over a family business after illness and after poor management had almost run it into the ground.

"You could change things, you know," she murmured.

His eyes snapped up to meet hers.

"You could," Hannah insisted more forcefully. She flashed him an encouraging smile. He cared about his family legacy. That was more than enough motivation to turn things around.

"Thanks for saying that. But I don't think so."

"I mean it," she insisted. "You can improve things. Turn this place around."

"You sound like my Dad."

"Then he's a very smart man," Hannah mused. She sipped at her hot chocolate. It was superb. It was so good she hadn't even yet considered what was on the menu.

"Yes, he is," Bruno answered. "The smartest man I know. It's just he can't take the pressure associated with the business anymore."

"Making one person happy is sometimes impossible, so I can't imagine making hundreds of them happy would be a walk in the park," she commented. "However, with even just a few small changes, things could be different. Get rid of the awful lighting for a start. And introduce some evening activities to entertain the visitors. There needs to be something to occupy them in the darkness too. Also, why does the kitchen at the lodge close so early? The chef leaves well before people get a chance to get good and hungry. And local flair," she added, warming to her theme. "You need artisans for specialty items only found here in these parts, not that carbon-copy plastic junk that's on sale now."

Hannah could have slapped her hand over her

mouth, but that would have been even more humiliating than her endless chatter.

Her tangents were going to get her into trouble if she didn't rein them in.

"Sorry," she said then. "Sometimes my tongue thinks it knows everything, and my brain is slow to catch up and tell it to shut up," she commented. She wanted to crawl under the table.

"No, keep going," Bruno said. He was leaning forward in his seat listening intently. "I think you have something there. Restoring the old lighting system *would* make things cheerier, and the artisans could give visitors something unique to remember us by. Maybe even something like a collection, so they get a new piece from here every time they visit?"

"Exactly!" Hannah smiled as a tingle of excitement rushed through her.

She loved all things Christmas, possibly because she'd never experienced the traditional picture postcard kind, and planning for the holidays was one of her favorite things to do.

"I like the idea of more activities in the evening. Things to keep guests entertained and even bring people together," Bruno continued, and Hannah could almost see the cogs in his mind turning now. "Maybe a show or something?"

"Absolutely." She sipped again at her chocolate. "I told you that you could turn this place around. Just doing those few things would make a huge improvement. More like what people expect when they come here." Then she laughed. "I should probably just make you a list."

The door to the back room of the café opened then, and Gretta came out. "You two ready to order?"

Hannah smiled at Bruno, who smiled back. "Not quite yet, Gretta, we actually got a bit lost in conversation," he chuckled. "Give us a couple more minutes?"

She nodded with a knowing smile. "Sure. Just holler and I'll come back out."

Hannah pulled the menu to her. "We better pick something though. I'm sure Gretta wants to close this place up."

"Nah," Bruno dismissed with a shrug. "She'd stay open all night as long as there's someone here. She likes the company. Usually, she's here alone testing recipes and prepping for the next day."

Hannah looked again at the door to the back. "Alone?"

"Yes. She doesn't have any family. Her son moved to Anchorage earlier this year. Things weren't going so well with the lull in visitors here, so he moved to help his family."

"Which means changing things around would do so much for the locals here too," she mused. "Make so many people's lives very different."

"You know … you say it like a joke, but I really think you should."

Hannah's eyes darted up. "Should what?"

"Make a list. I mean, I have to admit - I'm really no good with this stuff. I've lived here all my life, so I have no real idea what visitors expect. No idea how to create the fairytale Christmas experience people want. That *you* expected. So tell me."

Hannah sat back in her chair. She wanted to help him, but could her suggestions really make a difference? It's not as though she was any kind of expert in event planning or business; she was a photographer for goodness sake….

Then remembering, she looked balefully at her injured arm. "Well, it's not as though I have anything better to do …" she grimaced.

"And in exchange, I'll help *you* complete your assignment," Bruno told her, his eyes lighting up suddenly. "Let *me* be your right arm, maybe help you get those photos you need?" he continued, enthused afresh. "You can show me exactly what to do, and I can take the shots for you. That way we *both* win. I help you get the pictures you need for your assignment, and you help me turn this place around."

"I -"

"I know where to find the auroras," he blurted then, and Hannah's eyes widened.

"You do?"

"Of course. I've lived here my entire life, remember? Spent much of my childhood chasing the lights. I can take you to the best vantage points, and if you show me what to do, I can also make sure you get the best pictures for your work. You can still get the job done, and help out a community of struggling people at the same time. What do you say?"

Hannah's heart raced a little. It was a very interesting proposition.

She could still visualize her name under the shots in *Discover Wild,* maybe even a short editorial about her. The prospects it could mean for her career.

She bit her lip. *Could they really pull this off?*

"The best places?" she repeated.

Bruno smiled. "The very best."

"Alright. You have a deal. You make sure I get the most amazing pictures of the Northern Lights that anyone has ever seen, and I'll do my best to help you turn the tables on this town and put the magic back into Christmas World. Agreed?"

She extended her good hand toward him.

Bruno took it, and they shook firmly.

"Deal."

CHAPTER 16

She could already see the change in Bruno's eyes. It was as if she'd just shot him full of hope.

Their gazes remained on one another for several moments and Hannah felt her heart beat just a tad faster. She needed to do something before the silence made it explode.

"Um ... we better get something to eat," she muttered. "We have a lot of planning to do. That's always best on a full stomach."

"Good point."

Hannah looked over the menu while Bruno gave some suggestions on what to choose. She truly hoped she *could* help him now, though she wasn't sure how much they could really achieve in the short term.

But at least they could try.

Breakfast for dinner was highly underrated, but Hannah was a big fan. She plucked two fluffy pancakes from the serving plate and topped them with warm maple syrup, whipped cream, and fresh strawberries. Then added some strips of crispy bacon, three sausage links and hash browns.

"I like that," Bruno said smiling.

She looked up at him with a mouthful of pancake, then chewed it quickly and swallowed. "What?"

"A woman with a good appetite."

Hannah snorted as she laughed. "Yeah, I do like to eat." She enjoyed another mouthful. "I don't see the point in starving yourself. Your body needs food to fuel it, so you might as well enjoy it."

"I like the way you think. Sometimes I feel we overthink things in this world. Make it complicated just for the sake of it, as if it gives us some control."

"Life is short," Hannah replied. "And has so much to offer that we miss out worrying about stuff that's just trivial in the grand scheme, chasing things we don't care about because we have bills to pay. Starve ourselves of some really great food because we're worried about what we look like to people who don't even notice." She took another bite. "Don't get me wrong, of course you should aim to be healthy, but you don't need to starve yourself or eat boring food to do that."

"You sound like a spokeswoman for Jenny Craig or something," Bruno mused.

She chuckled. "No, just some of my late dad's wisdom."

"Another wise man?"

"Yep" she answered. "A very wise man. OK, so I guess I'll need to teach you the basics of using a camera."

"Don't you just point and shoot?"

She looked at him in dismay. "Tell me you're kidding."

"I'm kidding," he chuckled. "I know there's a lot more to it than that. There's a reason why we aren't all working for magazines."

Not everyone understood photography. They thought it was simple. You just magically found the perfect setting and took the shot.

But it took much more than that. It took

timing, lighting, the right angle and ... the perfect moment.

It wasn't something that just happened either. Sometimes you had to make it happen.

"We can work on that tomorrow, but for now let's make a start on *my* part of the bargain. And the first thing that needs to change in Christmas World is those tacky fluorescents," she scolded playfully. "They need to go - like, yesterday."

"Consider them gone," Bruno declared with a grin.

"Then we need to do something to improve the spirit of this place. It's supposed to be festive and cheery, but your elves are anything but. I don't think I've ever seen a more glum bunch in my entire life."

Bruno chuckled. "Cheer up the elves. Got it."

"And Santa too," she added, warming to her theme. "That guy *seriously* needs a makeover."

CHAPTER 17

The following days seemed to pass in a blur as Hannah and Bruno made plans and changes.

It was strange, but having improvements as her focus immediately helped brighten up the place's former atmosphere.

Suddenly, Christmas World had endless potential, and she, Hannah, was a part of it.

"How are things coming with the new lighting?" she asked, as she and Bruno ambled down a snowy main street together, while nearby, workmen were dismantling the overhead lights.

"The electrician promised me that everything will be good to go in time for tonight's s'mores roast," he informed. "We should have everything right on schedule."

"Excellent. That really will be the perfect thing to get the Christmas spirit flowing around here."

"The snowball throw isn't enough?" Bruno queried, chuckling.

The idea for a guest snowball throw involving locals and visitors had come to her a day after their impromptu dinner at Gretta's.

It was one of those cool wintery activities Hannah had always wanted to do; that, and make snow angels.

If she liked it she was sure others would too, and such an inclusive public event seemed the perfect way to mark the beginning of the big Christmas World turnaround.

In the meantime, Bruno had designed colorful fliers to announce some of the other festive happenings after they'd got the staff on board.

When they'd met with the staff Hannah had initially expected some protests, but she was surprised to find that they quite liked the boss's new ideas.

It got some of the staff members talking about their own favorite Christmas activities, which in turn, gave Bruno even more inspiration and incentive to transform the place once and for all.

Today was a light snow day. Hannah's hair was pulled into a high ponytail atop her head, and she was wearing a slightly lighter jacket now that she had grown more accustomed to the cold.

"Should we head over to the forest? It's almost time." She strolled beside Bruno with her camera slung over her shoulder.

Her wrist wasn't hurting as much as the first day; the medication from Dr. Morgan had helped a lot, as did the exercises.

She was supposed to wait a little bit longer before she used it, but was still impatient to get back to her photography.

"You want me to take that?" He reached for the camera strap.

"Thanks."

"Don't mention it," he replied. "After all, I'm the one who's supposed to be taking over. I figure this will be a good learning exercise."

"Yep," Hannah smiled. "Let's see what you can do."

THE WOODS AREA to the west of the town had been

transformed for tonight's first Christmas World Snowball Throw.

Mounds of pre-rolled snowballs were dotted between the trees.

It was one of the more fun tasks the staff had to do in years. Hannah couldn't join in to help, but had overseen the work and the positioning of the stacks earlier that afternoon.

Guests, staff and some locals were already gathered. They all stood around, not quite sure what do to, as she and Bruno approached.

She turned to him. "You're on, Mr. CEO."

He smiled nervously.

"You got this," Hannah whispered, patting his arm encouragingly. "Go get 'em."

She watched as Bruno walked into the midst of the gathered crowd. He raised a hand in greeting as he began to speak, and despite his smile, she knew he was inwardly terrified.

"Hey everyone, welcome to the inaugural Christmas World Snowball Throw. This year, we wanted to offer our visitors something new to do in our holiday town. We're changing it up and shaking things up, to ensure that you have the most memorable Christmas of your life."

The applause was small, but there were smiles on the faces of those gathered.

Hannah was sure some were a little skeptical of what was happening. People didn't often take sudden changes well, but in this case, it was all for the best.

This is going to work. I know it will.

CHAPTER 18

Hannah smiled as Bruno then sounded the charge for the fun to begin.

The moment the words were out of his mouth, elated screams and snowballs began to fly through the air in every direction.

She had to duck behind a tree to avoid getting caught in the crossfire and laughed as Bruno approached her, already covered in snow.

He'd gotten in a few early throws and some of his staff had returned the favor before he'd been able to make his retreat.

"What'd you think? A good start?" he laughed as he shook the snow from his golden hair.

"I'll say. Better get that camera ready," she replied. "You're also tonight's event photographer."

"Right." He took the Nikon from her and removed the lens cap.

"First, hold it up and get a feel for it. Then take a few candid shots."

"Of what?"

"Whatever you like, or whoever. I wanna see what kind of eye you have," she stated.

He looked at her with a cocked brow. "Alright. I'll give it a try." He turned to the volleys of snowballs and began snapping away.

At first, he didn't move around much, but as he got more into it his feet began to shift, he started adjusting the position of the camera in his hands, and she could see he was getting lost in the moment, zoning in on various groups of snowballers as they laughed and enjoyed themselves.

Hannah smiled. That was what she'd hoped for.

If Bruno could get comfortable with the camera on his own terms, not just taking direction from her, it would mean all the difference once they really got going.

Photography needed heart.

I can't give him mine, but I can at least try to tease out his.

She continued to watch him. The happier and

more confident he became with the shots he was taking, the more optimistic she felt.

By the time the snowball throw was over and it was time for the s'mores roast, she could tell that Bruno was really enjoying himself.

Now, the gaudy fluorescent lighting was gone, and strings of pretty white fairylights were draped on lampposts all the way round the town square. It looked magical.

Barbecue pits and s'mores stations had been established for visitors to gather their ingredients before taking everything to campfire pits and gather round.

Hannah took her camera back from Bruno as he collected food for them both.

In the meantime, she did her best to use one hand and take a few shots herself. They weren't great; they weren't even good, but still, they were something to capture the moment.

Tonight, for the first time since she'd got here, people in Christmas World looked cheery and festive, and more importantly, everyone was smiling.

It was the exactly the kind of atmosphere Hannah had been expecting, the kind of memorable moment she'd been hoping for when she first came here.

Then another idea struck her, and her eyes widened.

"What is it?" Bruno questioned as he returned to her with a teetering pile of marshmallows and chocolate.

"I've just thought of something; another improvement. How about a photo contest? Your most memorable Christmas World moment. Give everyone here the impetus to capture some fun moments for themselves while here … and they could also maybe win a prize of some sort? Entries could be posted on the notice board at Santa's Post Office and a winner announced at the end of every week."

"Where do you come up with these ideas? They're brilliant," he chuckled.

She grinned happily. "Hey I'm a photographer, remember? Capturing magic moments is what I do. And making them happen is what *you* do, or will be from now on," she teased.

"You know, I think you deserve something more than just a roasted s'more," Bruno mused.

"You have so many great ideas I can't keep up with them."

"Well, if you're offering, then maybe one of Gretta's legendary hot chocolates later?"

"I'll take you there after this."

"It's a date."

The words hung in the air, as he stared at her.

Oh your stupid mouth again, Hannah.

She laughed nervously. "You know what I meant. Not a date-date, just a…"

"No need to explain," Bruno replied, his expression unreadable but his eyes were twinkling. "Hot chocolate it is."

CHAPTER 19

In the days that followed, Christmas World began to become truly alive with the spirit of the season.

The change in mood was remarkable, so much so that it even drew Bruno's father back out into the holiday resort town he'd managed for most of his life.

Gerald Locke was slightly overweight with square-framed glasses and a salt-and-pepper beard that ran from his temples down his jaw and merged with his thick mustache.

His face was round and his hair was trimmed close to his head. He had a brilliant, jolly smile that made Hannah think of her dad when she saw him, even though they looked nothing alike.

And Santa of course.

"Evening, Mr Locke," Hannah greeted as she walked up to him in Gretta's.

He was at the same table where she and Bruno had come up with the idea to save Christmas World, and since that day they'd done most of their planning there.

Gretta seemed to love it, plus the increased clientele now coming through. Evening opening hours everywhere in the town had been extended, and once the visitors knew that, they came out in droves.

Though it didn't matter how busy the café was, Gretta made sure Hannah and Bruno's window table was always available for them.

"Hannah," the old man grumbled good-naturedly. "How many times must I tell you to call me Gerald?"

She smiled as she pulled out the seat beside him and lowered herself onto the chair.

"OK then, Gerald," she corrected. "You're looking great today."

"I feel great. It's nice to be out of retirement," he commented jokingly.

When Bruno had presented to the old Santa the idea of doing a full reindeer-led sleigh ride through town on Christmas Eve to distribute gifts to everyone, the current incumbent was immediately adamant that he wasn't going to do it.

He didn't like reindeer. He didn't like sleighs. He didn't like having to cry 'Ho-ho-ho' either.

Hannah couldn't fathom why the guy even had the job of being Santa in the first place. However, when Gerald had heard their plans, he immediately wanted to be a part of it.

Bruno had very quickly shared their ideas with his dad, and Mr Locke Senior had wanted to meet the woman who'd triggered all of these new changes.

Initially, Hannah had been nervous about meeting Bruno's dad, but at the same time, she was curious.

And was very pleasantly surprised.

The Locke men were the funniest when put together.

They were constantly teasing one another, rehashing old stories and laughing.

Dinner at Bruno's house was one of the most memorable evenings she'd had in a long time, and as all three talked about various other plans for Christmas World, Hannah found that she was liking the project more than she'd expected.

Initially, it had been a response to the obvious shortcomings of the holiday resort, but as she and Bruno had gotten further into the planning, and she could see how even the simplest changes were beginning to transform not only the town, but the people in it, it began to mean so much more.

It began to truly reflect what Christmas was about – community and togetherness.

It was also somewhat of a revelation for Hannah, who was used to remaining behind the lens, as opposed to being part of a scene.

She was so accustomed to experiencing things from afar, that it was actually somewhat overwhelming to now be right in the heart of all the excitement and fun.

And she was liking that bit far more than she'd anticipated.

Now, the door of the café opened and Bruno walked in.

A huge smile spread across Hannah's face at the sight of him.

It was completely involuntary, but the second she saw him it was like getting that Christmas gift you always wanted.

Stop it. Don't be silly. This is business.

She turned to find Gerald staring at her. "I think your assistant is here," he commented, biting into a cookie.

"Should you be eating that?" she chided.

"I'm getting into my role," Gerald replied. "What's a Santa who doesn't eat cookies?"

"Thinner," his son finished deadpan, and Hannah chuckled. Bruno turned to her. "Ready to go?"

"Got everything right here." She raised her camera bag.

"Perfect." He stepped around her chair and collected both her haversack and her camera bag from the floor beside her, before tossing both over his shoulders. "Time to shoot for the stars."

CHAPTER 20

Most of all, Hannah loved their nights beneath the sky.

Bruno really had been true to his word; he knew all the best vantage points for the Northern Lights, and now he sat beside her on the sled as they stared in awe at the radiating colors.

"Every night really is different," she commented breathlessly, as bands of ethereal green danced in the sky above them.

"I know," Bruno smiled. "That's what's great about it. You never know what to expect."

"Could you imagine seeing this every day?"

Bruno's pale green eyes seemed to radiate with a light of their own under the magnetic rays. "Yes, because I do."

Hannah laughed as she looked back at him. "Of course."

"Having someone to share it with makes it different, though," he added gently. "I'm glad you're here."

"So am I."

Her heart fluttered.

Stop it, Hannah. It's not like that. He's just holding up his part of the deal.

Every day she had to remind herself that what was between her and Bruno was purely business.

However, the more time she spent with him alone, together beneath the stars, the more difficult it was for her to come to terms about that fact.

She looked back up at the sky. "So now, get the shot in frame…" she instructed.

Bruno duly manoeuvred the camera lens back up and began to take more photos.

It was the best way to distract herself.

The more Hannah focused on work, the less she could think of Bruno Locke or the way his eyes made her want to look into them every single day. Nor the stir of her heart when she did.

He set the camera aside again after a few minutes.

"Pass me the coffee from my bag?" He leaned

over to fetch the rucksack himself, having realized it was on the same side as her bad arm.

In the meantime, Hannah had reached across to grab the flask with her good hand, and turned back, only to meet him midway.

Their noses practically touched, and her breath caught at their proximity. Her gaze met his and she thought Bruno seemed as affected by their closeness as she did, but for some reason, neither of them moved.

They just stayed there, staring into each other's eyes.

Hannah's heart began to dance in her chest as her breath quickened.

"Bruno?" she whispered, after what felt like forever.

"Yes?"

"Here's your coffee."

She watched him swallow the lump in his throat, and he blinked several times before sitting back as he reached for the flask. "Thanks."

"You're welcome."

"Maybe we should head back soon," he suggested as he set the flask aside unopened. "It's getting late."

"Good idea," she replied distractedly, still a little discombobulated.

What was happening? It felt as if her skin was magnetized, it was tingling so much and her heart still hadn't calmed.

He got to his feet first, and helped her up after him, before starting to pack up the equipment.

Hannah wanted to help, but he insisted that she should just get herself comfortable on the sled for the journey back, and she duly began to move some stuff to make more room.

Bruno's rucksack was still open, so she went to zip it back up, until something inside caught her eye.

Some words on a white page inside.

Her curiosity piqued, she looked back to where he was still packing up their stuff, before pulling the document out further, scanning it quickly.

It was a property sale agreement … For Christmas World.

Hannah's galloping heart stopped for a moment as her eyes moved to the bottom of the page.

Signed and dated by Bruno.

CHAPTER 21

Hannah could hardly look at him since, she felt so betrayed.

He'd made her believe he wanted to turn things around for Christmas World, but he'd already signed the documents to sell it.

Why was he wasting her time - and everyone else's?

She felt like a fraud walking amongst the resort staff now, seeing their optimistic faces and hearing their excited chatter about all of the changes so far.

Knowing that it was all a lie. Their boss was a liar and even worse, she was his accomplice.

It isn't your business, Hannah.

Christmas World is Bruno's and if he wants to sell it what does it have to do with you?

He can do whatever he wants. So what if he used you to make things better. He probably just made those improvements to make the place more attractive to buyers.

You were just too blinded by charisma and good-looks to notice. You should know better.

Things aren't always what they seem.

Now at the lodge, Hannah sat on the edge of her bed and mulled over the discovery that had been plaguing her ever since she'd happened across the truth.

Should she just leave now without saying anything, or should she confront him?

She picked up her scarf and wrapped it around her neck. Bruno and Gerald were expecting her at the café today.

They were seated at their usual table, but Hannah didn't have the same warm feeling she'd grown accustomed to at seeing them.

Now she looked at Bruno and felt only disappointment.

At both him and herself.

But for his dad's sake, she did her best to hide it.

"Hannah, Dad and I were just talking about the photo competition. Submissions finished today, so now we just need to check the entries and declare a winner. I was thinking you and I could do that after Gretta closes up for the day? Everything else is pretty much all set up and ready for the Big Night," Bruno added, referring to the upcoming Santa Departure celebrations; the culmination of all the changes they'd already made.

He was grinning like the cat that swallowed the canary.

"Oh," she replied. "About that," she began. "I won't actually be here for the Christmas Eve party after all."

"Why not, Hannah?" Gerald asked, concerned. "Has something happened?"

"I've just decided that it's high time I got home."

"But I thought you were going to stay on till after Christmas?" Bruno questioned. "After all the hard work you put in, surely you'd want to be here to celebrate with everyone. The pinnacle of all your wonderful ideas. You can't miss that, Hannah. I mean, what about…" Then he trailed off, as if about to say something else, but thinking better of it.

She glared at him. How could he talk about

celebrating, given what he was planning to do as soon as everything was over?

Were the new buyers going to be there on Christmas Eve? Would they be coming out just to see how 'special' the place could be?

Then she thought of something else. Had Bruno signed the deal with them before or after he'd dazzled Hannah with the aurora borealis?

"I don't have to be there. This is for the people who belong here."

"But it wouldn't be anything without you," Gerald countered. "You made it all possible."

She forced a smile. "Thank you, Gerald, but I'm sure Bruno would have come up with something on his own. I just gave him a nudge in the right direction."

"It was more than a nudge," he protested. "You inspired all of this - everything."

Hannah felt her eyes sting. *Don't remind me.*

"Hey, there is something wrong," Bruno pressed. He was looking at her keenly and she did everything she could to avoid his gaze.

"Bruno," his dad said calmly. "If Hannah needs to go she needs to go." Gerald smiled at her. "We were very lucky to have her and her ideas to help us out," he continued. "But we can't keep her forever, and she has her own life back in California."

Hannah swallowed in an attempt to clear the thickening in her throat.

"That's right. I've got everything I needed for my assignment. Now, I need to go home."

Bruno pushed away from the table and got to his feet. "Excuse me."

She watched as he left the café without another word.

He's acting hurt, but it's not his emotion to feel.

He's the one who lied. The one who tricked, who betrayed everyone.

Hannah folded her arms over her chest.

She couldn't wait to get on that plane and home to reality.

Things weren't so magical anymore in Christmas World.

CHAPTER 22

She stayed on with Gerald in the cafe for a bit while they had lunch together. If Bruno wanted to sulk or get upset it was his business.

It had nothing to do with her.

Nothing here has anything to do with me. I came for a job. I got my photos, that's all I came for.

Nothing more.

It was later when Bruno returned with the photo competition entry box. The café was by then quieter and Gretta was out back preparing for the evening trade.

The older woman had since confided that things had turned around so much that if it continued, her son might even be able to leave his job in Anchorage and come back home.

Hannah hoped she wouldn't be disappointed. Who knew what the new owners would do with the place once they took over?

"Will you help with these before you go?" Bruno asked her tersely, as he put the box on the table between her and Gerald. "It's kind of your speciality after all."

She barely looked at him. "Sure."

There were dozens of entries, and as the three sorted through all the happy Christmas World memories captured by families and couples over the last week or so, Hannah felt even more disheartened.

"So much to choose from," she mused. "How can we possibly pick a winner?"

"Well, *I* think it's obvious," Gerald smiled, staring at the photograph he was holding.

He looked over at Bruno. "Yours wins hands down, son."

"What?" Hannah asked, surprised. "Bruno entered a photo?"

He looked at her sheepishly. "I did," he replied. "I wanted it to be a surprise."

"And you think it should win?" she asked

Gerald in disbelief. OK, so she'd taught Bruno a lot about photography, but she couldn't see how it could be *that* good.

Then Gerald slid the picture in her direction and Hannah stared in disbelief.

It was a candid shot of her beneath the night sky; her face illuminated by the Northern Lights as she stared in awe at the spectacle.

The pure wonder in her expression was deeply vivid, so much so that at the time, Hannah never even realized that Bruno had turned the lens on her.

She was shocked to see how well he'd captured the emotion she was feeling just then. He made her look … radiant. The way any photographer who truly cared about his subject might.

Now, her gaze rose to meet Bruno's. How could he take a picture like that and lie to her all this time?

How could the photo suggest the kind of affection and respect that the things he'd done belied?

What was real?

"I … have to go," she muttered, suddenly.

Hannah rushed out of the café, unable to say any more. She slipped her arms into her jacket, but didn't let the action slow her pace. She needed to get as far away from Bruno (and that picture) as possible.

"Hannah," a voice called out from behind her then.

She turned to find his dad struggling to catch up in the snow and she slowed immediately. "Gerald?"

"Thank you for stopping," the older man said. "I was afraid I'd have to run after you to catch up. You'd be back at the lodge by the time I managed it," he chuckled.

"I wouldn't run away from you," she said fondly.

"I know," he replied. "What I don't know is why you're running at all."

Her expression was guarded. "What do you mean?"

"You raced out of there as if wild dogs were after you," he mused. "Something's going on Hannah. I want to know what's wrong."

She shook her head. "It's nothing. I just need to go home."

He looked at her. "You know, don't you?"

"Know what?"

"About the sale," he stated and Hannah's heart dropped to her toes.

"You know about that?" she asked, incredulously.

Gerald's gaze fell for a moment. "Of course. Bruno signed the contract a couple of weeks ago, but I asked him for one last Christmas to see if things turned around before I co-signed," he admitted. "He can't sign away Christmas World without me, you see."

Then he met her eyes and smiled. "I hoped something would happen to change things - a Christmas miracle of sorts. And I was right," he continued happily. "You appeared. You inspired my son and look at what's happened!" He gestured around the enlivened town square. "Bruno finally has a vision for this place - his vision, not mine or my father's or grandfather's. You gave him confidence to keep our legacy going. *You* were the change we all so badly needed." He plucked her chin lightly, while she tried to get to grips with what she was hearing. "Hannah, you were exactly the little piece of Christmas magic I was holding out for."

CHAPTER 23

Hannah couldn't move. She could hardly think.

What was Gerald saying? Were they selling Christmas World or not?

"I assure you, Bruno has no intention of selling this place now," the older man confirmed. "Neither do I. This Christmas will be the best we've had here in a long time, and I anticipate many more to come."

"And we have you to thank for that, Hannah," Bruno interrupted gently.

She hadn't noticed him approach, but now he was standing a few feet away from them.

Gerald turned to his son and smiled. "I think I can leave you to explain the rest," he stated, then turned and began to shuffle slowly back toward the café.

Hannah remained motionless. She'd spent the past couple of days slowly growing to resent Bruno, but now she was hearing that she was wrong about him, about everything.

She still wasn't sure she believed it, though.

"Hannah," he began, as he took slow steps toward her, the way she herself approached wildlife to photograph, so as not to frighten them into running.

Was that what Bruno felt? Was he afraid she'd run away?

Her heart was racing. She watched as he grew closer and part of her wanted to leave, but another part needed to stay and hear him out.

She wanted to be wrong about what she'd come to believe. She wanted there to be more than what she was telling herself.

"I didn't want to tell you about the sale," Bruno stated gently. "Or admit that I'd given up on this place long before I met you. I was just holding on for my dad's sake, hoping to get through this one last season before we gave it all up for good." He stepped closer. "I didn't have a vision before. I didn't believe I could turn things around. I didn't even know how."

Hannah swallowed her galloping heart.

"I thought selling was the best thing to do. It would allow Dad to have an easy life, no stress from running this place and enough money to take care of his retirement." Bruno sighed. "Better than running our family's legacy into the ground. Then I met you," he continued, taking a final step toward her. "And everything changed. You changed everything - for me."

"Bruno…"

"When I saw Christmas World through your eyes, Hannah, it opened mine," he continued, undeterred. "Your disappointment and your vision, it helped me to see that this wasn't just about business - it was about the people who come here to have a magical, once in a lifetime festive experience. It wasn't even about the family legacy, it was about what my great-grandfather originally wanted, a place where people could experience the real joy of Christmas."

"That's really great, Bruno. I'm glad you found your way. I told you that you would," she replied guardedly. "But what does it have to do with me?"

"Everything," he insisted reaching for her good hand. "It means everything."

Hannah searched his eyes as he continued to speak. Her ears could hardly believe what she was hearing.

Bruno's thumbs caressed the back of her wrist and her heart danced at the sensation.

This his hand released hers and rose to her cheek, until he held her face gently. "Do you know why I took that picture, Hannah?"

"No," she whispered. "I don't even know *when* you took it."

He smiled. "You were so lost in the auroras, in that magic they create that you didn't notice when I turned the camera away from the lights to you. I had to capture you, to hold on to you - and that moment. I didn't know if I'd ever get another chance, so I took it."

"Another chance to do what?" Hannah asked.

She was shocked that the words were even able to come out of her mouth. Her tongue seemed to have stopped working somewhere along the way from when Bruno started to talk until this moment.

He stifled a laugh. "You had me the first day I met you, did you know that?"

She shook her head.

"The moment I saw you standing there in the snow waving at me, calling out. Then, even when you started grumbling about Christmas World, I realized you were someone I wanted to know better," he continued. "The more I got to know, the more I wanted to know, and the more I didn't want you to leave. But I knew I couldn't keep you here either. I knew you were here for a reason, and once that was over you'd leave - so I had to hold on to what I could. Immortalize how I felt, I guess."

She thought her heart was going to crash out of her chest it was beating so loudly against her ribs.

Hannah sucked in a deep breath. "I thought I was the only one who was feeling that," she whispered. "I tried to pretend I didn't."

Bruno's hands slid down the side of her neck and settled on her shoulders.

"I couldn't hide it any longer," he stated as his arms closed gently around her and he pulled her closer. "I tried. I really did. I wanted to pretend I didn't feel the way I do, but I can't deny it, Hannah. That's why I entered the picture in the competition. I couldn't tell you how I felt, so I thought that …maybe I could *show* you. Especially after our last night out there, beneath the stars." He smiled. "I really wanted to kiss you then, you know."

"Why didn't you?" she asked but her throat was so dry she could hardly hear her own voice.

There was no fighting the irresistible tug between them and Hannah didn't need to, not when she knew Bruno felt the same for her as she did for him.

"Because I didn't know if you'd want me to. Hannah, you don't know how much I struggled not to when you were so close. All I had to do was lean forward an inch and touch your lips with mine…"

She allowed herself to melt into him, losing all thought of anything else as she savored the warmth of his breath amidst the cold night air.

"… like this."

Before finally, Bruno's lips met hers.

CHAPTER 24

❄

Later, the two of them stood again out on the tundra, watching another truly spectacular aurora display.

Shimmering green zigzagged through the sky in wondrous illumination, as Hannah stood wrapped in the warmth of Bruno's arms.

"So have you decided then?" he whispered in her ear from behind. His lips caressed her earlobe as he spoke, and she felt a tingle run up her spine.

"Decided what?" she replied nonchalantly.

He chuckled. "You know," he asked nuzzling at her cheek. "What's it going to be? Will you stay here for Christmas and enjoy the changes you've wrought to this town, and my life, or are you going to disappear back to California and forget all about us?"

Hannah's heart stuttered. She took a deep breath and turned to face him.

"I came here with one mission – get great shots of the aurora borealis, and the job of my dreams. But to be honest, being forced to step away from the lens for a while kind of made me realize how much I hide away from being a part of what's going on around me."

He looked confused. "But you travel all over with your photography. You're constantly in the middle of things."

"Not really," she explained. "Yes, I go out looking for the perfect picture. But I never let myself be in it. Here, I got the chance to step out from behind the camera and be part of the scene, as it were."

Bruno smiled, pulling her even closer. He smelled of aftershave, dark chocolate and mint. She rested her head on his chest.

"Well, clearly you are talented on both sides. We already have repeat bookings for next year, and some of the artisans have even approached me about getting their store space back once I reduced the prices."

Hannah looked up at him. "I told you, you could do it."

"Only because I had you to help me. I don't know if I really could've done it without you."

"Of course you could."

"No," he countered. "I mean it. You made all the difference." He gazed into her eyes. "Anyway I'm not sure I'd *want* to do it without you," he continued.

She looked at him. "What do you mean?"

He ran his fingers through his hair. "I know I should give you time, but I'm saying straight out, that I don't want you to go, Hannah," Bruno answered. "I'm saying that I've fallen for you and I'd love the chance to see if maybe there's something more here than just a Christmas romance ..."

She wasn't breathing. She couldn't breathe. It was crazy. They barely knew each other.

But then why was she smiling so much?

"Bruno, this is very sudden," she replied as she tried to catch her breath.

"I know. But I'm just telling you that I know how *I* feel. I don't play games, Hannah. I'm not built that way," he continued. "I believe there's more than a chance for us, but I can't do it alone. I know you'll get the job with the magazine, but how about shooting for the stars with me too?"

She smiled, not so confident about her prospects with *Discover Wild,* but even if she did get the job, as a freelancer she could still work from anywhere.

"So let me get this straight, you're offering me the chance to stay in a snow-filled winter wonderland where it's Christmas every day, and every night you get to watch the world's most magical natural phenomenon beneath a starlit sky... every photographer's dream?"

He was grinning from ear-to-ear. "So does that mean..."

Hannah closed her eyes and lost herself in the moment, one she suspected would be the first of many.

She'd come here for an assignment but was staying for love, not just for Bruno, but to be part of a this place, a community that truly did make dreams come true and opened up magical possibilities in the everyday.

Here, she could experience that wonder all the time, plus a chance at the kind of happiness she'd never known.

"I'm staying," she told him, smiling as he kissed her. "For Christmas, and as long as you'll have me."

From the Author:

Thanks for reading CHRISTMAS BENEATH THE STARS. I very much hope you enjoyed it.

If you're still in a festive reading mode, you might enjoy 12 DOGS OF CHRISTMAS, another festive tale from me, out now.
Read on for a short excerpt.

Thanks again!
Melissa xx

12 DOGS OF CHRISTMAS - EXCERPT

Animal lover Lucy feels blessed with her dream job; walking other people's dogs for a living. The pooches she cares for are her closest friends - as good as family, and Lucy would concede that she certainly understands them a lot more than people.

She wouldn't admit to having favourites among her charges, but if she really had to choose, it would be Berry; a humongous, fun-loving Labradane who never stops eating.

One day, a week before Christmas, when dropping Berry back to his elderly owner, Lucy is immediately concerned when there's no reply.

Until a neighbour breaks the news that sadly the old woman has died.

And when absent relatives quickly make it clear that the dog is not their problem, Lucy realises she's the only one left to take care of Berry.

Her landlord won't let her take him in - even temporarily - so in order to help the big dog find a home in time for the holidays, Lucy needs to push herself out of her comfort zone and into the community in her quest to find Berry his perfect match.

Soon realising that at this time of year, maybe it's not just dogs, but people, who need rescuing too.

CHAPTER 1

The curtains were wide open when Lucy Adams woke up. She must have forgotten to close them the night before, and now she was glad for that.

Snow outlined the windowsill like a frame, and the blanketed San Juan Mountains - the sun just peeking above its summit - was the picture.

It was a beautiful sight to wake up to.

She sighed happily. Small town life was very different to what it had been like in Denver, but she should have known the city wasn't for her.

Lucy was a Whitedale native, born and bred.

Once upon a time, she thought that time in the big city would help her shyness, and allow her to live out her grandmother's dream of her becoming a success.

Gran had been so sure that Lucy becoming an investigative journalist and seeing her name on the by-line of a story would have spurred her on to even greater things, but it didn't.

Because she never got any further than being a fact-checker.

Lucy was crippingly shy; always had been. When she was a child her mother tried everything to help bring her out of her shell, but it was no use.

Her timidity and innate reserve around people made it difficult for her to even broach the subject of an article to her boss.

In the end, she realized that no matter how hard she tried, she'd never be as happy in Denver as she would be back home.

So home she came.

Now, she swung her legs from beneath the sheets and did a few quick stretches to loosen herself up for the day ahead. Then quickly made her bed; the wrinkled sheets and pillow depressed on only one side.

Her apartment was the best she could afford; a small upper-level two-bed on Maypole Avenue, close to all the parks and trails.

When she started renting it a couple of years ago, she'd sort of hoped that by now she'd have someone to share it with, but no such luck.

Lucy didn't know why, but she seemed to have been born without the romance gene too.

She knew she wasn't bad looking, with her shoulder-length caramel-colored hair and fair skin. Her smile was big and warm, but the problem likely was that she didn't really smile around people.

Animals yes; humans not so much.

People made her nervous, which was why having a dog-walking business was a plus. Lucy spent her days surrounded entirely by those who understood her without judgment.

Lucy was very proud of her business, 12 Dogs Walking Service. It was the premier dog-walking outfit in town, and she had dreams of making it even better.

Once she had enough money saved and found the right location, she fully intended to add other services, like doggie daycare and pet pampering.

She envisioned her little business as one day being the best animal care center in the county, if not the state.

But hey, one day at a time.

The wooden floors were cool beneath her feet as Lucy left her bedroom and walked into the kitchen.

She fixed herself a bowl of cereal and a cup of coffee while waiting for her computer to wake.

She loved her trusty old-model Dell PC, but Betsy was on her last legs. It used to take less than a minute for it to boot up, now it was more like seven.

Lucy hummed the lyrics to *Must Have Been the Mistletoe* as she got out her apple cinnamon granola and almond milk. She did her best to eat well, and in Whitedale that was made easier by the popularity of the farm-to-table movement.

Then she settled at her two-seater dining table by the small window overlooking the square.

The town was slowly coming to life - in a few hours, cars and people would be bustling along the streets, but for the moment it was just store owners looking for an early start, and a few joggers out for a morning run.

When the PC was fully loaded, the home screen flickered to life, and a picture of a golden-haired cocker spaniel greeted Lucy, making her smile immediately.

"So let's see what's going on today..." she mumbled as she opened her emails; a couple of subscription updates to animal magazines and journals, and a few more notifying her of pet trade shows in the area.

Then requests from her clients.

Bob St. John wanted Blunders walked on Thursday. He was a new client and Blunders, a three-year-old dachshund, was sorely in need of Lucy's services.

Bob, loving owner that he was, had been won over by Blunder's pleading looks, and now the dog was carrying a little too much weight. The extra pounds for a larger breed might've been easier to handle, but the dachshund's long body made it more easily prone to herniated discs.

The sooner Blunders got the exercise in, and if Bob stuck to the diet the vet had recommended, Lucy was sure that the little dog would be fine in no time.

"Dear Bob ..." she intoned out loud, as she began to type a response confirming the date and time, and set an alert reminder for herself on her phone.

Martha Bigsby wanted Charlie walked every day that week. Charlie was a six-year-old Airedale Terrier. His coat was perfect and thankfully so was his health. He was Martha's prize-winning pooch and she loved him dearly.

Lucy loved owners who shared her appreciation for their animals. Charlie had a big show coming up before the holidays, and she wanted to be sure he was ready for it.

Dear Martha. I confirm that I'll pick up Charlie at seven each morning this week. We can return to our normal nine o'clock slot once you're back from Bakersfield.

She spent the next twenty minutes replying to her work emails before checking her personal ones, though was finished with those in less than one.

Lucy's life consisted mostly of work, and very little of the social aspects that most other people found entertaining. Socialising just wasn't her thing really.

She'd always been happier around animals than people. They, especially dogs, were easy to understand and predictable for the most part.

People weren't, and that was a difficulty for

Lucy. She liked what she could rely on and she'd been disappointed far too many times by people.

Never by her furry friends.

Her phone rang then and she checked the caller display. It was Eustacia, her neighbor on the floor below; a woman who believed it was her job to marry off every singleton in their building.

"Lucy? Are you there? Of course, you're there. You're screening my calls aren't you?" Eustacia's Brooklyn accent pierced her ears.

Her new neighbor, who had moved from New York four months ago, was convinced she knew what was best for Lucy, and that she'd find her the 'perfect guy'.

"Trust me. I know all about these things. At home, they used to call me the matchmaker. I can set up anyone with anyone. You leave it to me. A young girl like you shouldn't be all alone every night. It's ain't natural."

Lucy would've appreciated the help, if it weren't for the fact that Eustacia had terrible taste in men.

"Mrs. Abernathy in 4C told me that her son Martin is back in town. And I told her you'd love to meet him. Would you give her a call? She says he'd loved to meet you too."

A perfect example of Eustacia's poor taste: Martin Abernathy was four years older than Lucy. He had a habit of snorting all the time and when she was little, he used to stick gum in her hair.

She rolled her eyes as her neighbor's shrill voice continued. She washed the dishes and put them away, and Eustacia was *still* talking.

Then, finally making her excuses, Lucy hung up the phone and got ready for work.

Her clothing and shoes were comfortable, cosy and most importantly, breathable. There was a *lot* of walking around in her line of work, and no matter what the deodorant companies claimed, she'd rather be safe than sorry.

Dogs were after all, very sensitive to smell.

CHAPTER 2

First, Lucy headed to Olympus Avenue, where one of her charges resided.

While the service was called 12 Dogs, in truth she rarely had as many pooches all at once, but could certainly handle that much.

She also didn't do favorites, and would never admit to having one. Much like people, breeds were individual, and to say you liked dog one better than the other was somewhat unfair. People couldn't help who they were and neither could animals.

However, if Lucy *truly* had to choose a favorite dog – and was absolutely pressed on the matter – she'd pick Berry Cole.

Berry was a five-year-old chocolate brown Labrador and Great Dane mix – a Labradane.

Lucy just called him a sweetie.

He was loyal and loving, and despite his humongous size, being closer in build to his Great Dane mother than his Lab father, he was very gentle.

He was also the perfect choice for his owner, Mrs Cole. Though Lucy sometimes wondered how the seventy-five-year-old woman managed to feed the colossus.

He was *always* hungry, so much so that Lucy had started carrying extra snacks soon after he'd joined her troop.

Though if she could pick a dog for herself, it couldn't be one as huge as Berry. But that was a moot point, because unfortunately, Lucy's landlord didn't allow pets in the building.

Mrs. Cole was a widow with no children, and Lucy sometimes wondered if that would be her own fate - a life alone. Though at least Mrs. Cole had a canine companion. She didn't even have that.

Now she knocked on the door.

"Morning," Mrs. Cole greeted Lucy with a smile the moment she opened the door. She looked tired today, more so than on most mornings when she called to pick up Berry.

Maybe she was feeling down.

Lucy could bring her back something from Toasties to perk up her spirits. It was the best cafe and pastry store in all of Whitedale, and Mrs. Cole had a thing for their Peppermint Chocolate Croissants.

"Hi, Mrs. Cole. Is he ready?" The words came out in a plume of white. Winter was well and truly here and Christmas now only a couple of weeks away.

They'd had their first heavy snowfall just a few days before and soon, the entirety of Whitedale would be covered in it.

The words had only just left Lucy's mouth, when the big dog came bounding to the door. He rushed past his owner and promptly jumped up and landed his big paws on her chest, knocking her back a step.

"Berry, calm down," Mrs. Cole scolded lightly.

"It's okay," Lucy laughed as Berry licked her face. "He's just happy to see me."

The older woman chuckled. "He always is. I can't contend with him like I used to with this hip.

I'm so happy he still gets to go out and have fun when you're around."

"It's my pleasure, and you know I really love this big guy," Lucy chuckled as she removed his paws from her chest and stooped down to scratch behind his ears.

Mrs. Cole duly handed her the leash from by the door and Lucy clipped it in place. She carried spare leashes and clean-up items in her backpack, but it was important to get Berry on the right track from the get-go.

"He's staying out for the whole day, yes?" she confirmed.

"Yes, if that's good with you."

Mrs. Cole was one of the few people Lucy could chat easily to. She supposed it was because she reminded her so much of the grandmother who had raised her.

She didn't have anyone now though. A fact she was well used to, but whenever Christmas came around, it was just that little bit harder to bear.

"Of course. You have a great day," Lucy told Mrs Cole as she began to lead Berry from the porch. "And get back inside, it's cold out. We'll see you later."

"You too," the older woman called after her, chuckling as Lucy struggled to keep pace with the dog. "And don't let the big guy wear you out too much."

CHAPTER 3

The feeling of Christmas was well and truly in the air.

All the stores in town were now fully decorated for the holiday season. Garlands and wreaths were everywhere, twinkling lights in every shop window, and the local tree farm business was booming with a fine selection of firs, pines and spruces.

Lucy wasn't getting a tree though. She never did. It felt wasted when it was just her.

She stopped for a moment to look into the window of Daphne's Dreamland Toy store, smiling automatically at the holiday display. The place was every child's wonderland and had been in existence for over forty years.

Lucy could remember when her mother used to bring her there as a child. The owner, Daphne would give her candy canes whenever she came in.

She was gone now though, just like Lucy's mother.

A deep sadness filled her heart at the memory. Her mom had been a lone parent and her dad was in the military.

They married before being deployed but he never came back. He sent her mother annulment papers a few months later. He'd met someone else where he was stationed and decided that she was the better choice.

Her mother had never quite gotten over it.

A sudden jerk snapped Lucy back to the present as Berry resumed his march toward home.

It was now a little after four in the afternoon, when she usually dropped the dogs back.

Berry was her final drop-off today, and he seemed to know it was past time, because he was trotting toward Olympus so purposefully that she knew only the prospect of food could be drawing him.

"Hey, slow down there, buddy," she commanded gently. "We'll be there soon."

She'd never seen him so determined. It was strange.

"Wait. I'm coming, I'm coming," Lucy called as he rushed to the corner and made a beeline for the street. He jerked hard and she almost tripped on the curb as the leash slipped from her hand, and the big dog ran off.

He disappeared down the street and she rushed after him.

"Hey there big guy ..." Lucy heard a voice call out from nearby, and rushing round to Mrs Cole's, she stopped short.

A man, over six feet tall and dressed in jeans, a red plaid shirt, brown jacket and a hardhat, was standing outside the house.

Lucy had never seen him before, but clearly, Berry had.

The dog's paws were planted solidly on the man's chest and he was licking his face eagerly, as his tail wagged behind him. The guy, whoever he was, was laughing heartily at the affection.

Lucy watched the friendly moment like an intruder.

"Hey buddy, where's your mama today, huh? Where is she?" he was asking in a sing-song tone.

It was several seconds before he noticed her

and turned to meet her gaze, but when he did Lucy's breath hitched.

He was so handsome. Square jaw with a dimple in his chin. A five o'clock shadow, tanned skin and the most brilliant blue eyes she'd ever seen. He wasn't any Martin Abernathy that was for sure. She could see dark brown hair peeking out from beneath the hardhat.

"Hello," he greeted with a smile, then nodded toward the house. "You looking for Mrs. Cole, too?"

Lucy couldn't speak for several seconds. She just stared at him. This was what always happened when handsome men spoke to her; she completely lost all sense. Her shyness took over and suddenly she became an incoherent nincompoop, her mind completely muddled.

Finally, she found her tongue before she embarrassed herself any further.

"Yes, returning Berry. I'm his dog walker."

He looked at her blankly for a second, and then smiled. "Oh. Are you Lucy?"

She was shocked that he knew her name.

"Yes …" she stammered. "Who are you?"

He took several steps to close the gap between them and extended his hand with a dazzling smile.

"I'm Scott. Mrs. Cole's contractor. I just finished working on her roof."

Lucy took his hand. "I didn't know she had one," she replied.

"A roof?"

A second of anxiety struck her. "No ... a contractor."

He chuckled. "I was just kidding."

Well done Lucy. Next time, try something simple like 'nice to meet you'.

"Nice to meet you," she mumbled.

"Nice to finally meet you too," he replied as he drew his hand back. He looked at the house and then back to her. "Was she expecting you back now?"

Finally? What did that mean? Did he know her from somewhere? She was certain he couldn't. She'd certainly never seen him before.

Maybe Mrs. Cole had mentioned her. But why?

"Yes. I always bring Berry back around this time. When he stays out all day," she added quickly, when she realized that she hadn't answered.

Berry himself was already at the door scratching to be let in. As always the big guy was ravenous.

"Strange," Scott stated as he turned back to her. "I've been here for a while now, and she hasn't answered. I usually check in on her when I can. I don't like that she's all alone in winter, especially given the darker nights and cold weather. So I try to stop by now and again, just to make sure she's okay."

How sweet.

"She's probably just late getting back from the store or something," he shrugged.

But that didn't make sense to Lucy. Mrs. Cole always made sure she was home when they got there.

She knew how Berry got by that hour of the day. His mind was solely on his dinner and if he didn't get it he got grumpy.

Something wasn't right.

"I have to go," Scott said then. "I've got a meeting with a client over on Hilliard. Could you tell her I stopped by and I'll pass back soon?"

Lucy nodded. "Sure." She turned and watched him walk back to his truck.

Berry attempted to follow him but Lucy grabbed a hold of his leash as he tried to gallop off. "Oh no, you don't Buster. Not this time."

Scott got into the truck and then turned back

to wave in their direction as he drove off. "See you around, Lucy."

She waved back, still slightly dazed by the unexpected encounter. "See you around."

End of Excerpt.

12 DOGS OF CHRISTMAS is out now in paperback & digital.

ABOUT THE AUTHOR

USA Today & international #1 bestselling author Melissa Hill lives in Dublin. Her page-turning contemporary stories are published worldwide and translated into 25 different languages.

Multiple titles are in development for movies and TV, including a Netflix series and an adaptation project with Reese Witherspoon's production company, Hello Sunshine.

A GIFT TO REMEMBER movie is currently airing on Hallmark Channel US, or Sky Cinema in UK/Ireland and THE CHARM BRACELET movie is filming for Christmas, 2020.

A movie adaptation of CHRISTMAS BENEATH THE STARS is in development for 2021.

www.melissahill.ie

ALSO BY MELISSA HILL

Author Page
Something You Should Know
Not What You Think
Never Say Never
Wishful Thinking
All Because of You
The Last to Know
Before I Forget
Please Forgive Me
The Truth About You
Something From Tiffany's
The Charm Bracelet
The Guest List
A Gift to Remember
The Hotel on Mulberry Bay
A Diamond from Tiffany's
The Gift of A Lifetime
Keep You Safe

The Summer Villa

Printed in Great Britain
by Amazon